T5-CRD-553

ROTARY
INTERNATIONAL
Donated in
honor of
CARMEN M. ORTIZ
United States Attorney
Guest Speaker
Quincy Rotary Club
Mar 20, 2012

Explore Outer Space

Venus

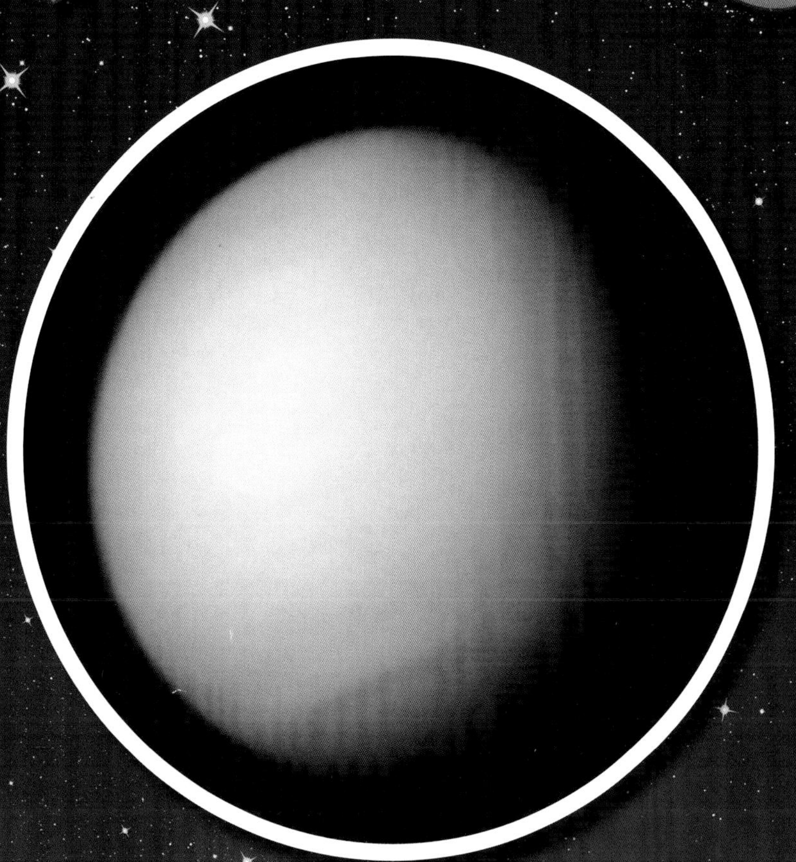

by Ruth Owen

New York

Published in 2014 by Windmill Books, An Imprint of Rosen Publishing
29 East 21st Street, New York, NY 10010

Produced for Windmill by Ruby Tuesday Books Ltd
Editor for Ruby Tuesday Books Ltd: Mark J. Sachner
US Editor: Sara Howell
Designer: Emma Randall
Consultant: Kevin Yates, Fellow of the Royal Astronomical Society

Photo Credits:
Cover, 1, 10–11, 13, 14–15, 16 (bottom), 21, 22–23, 24–25, 26–27 © NASA; 4–5, 6–7, 8–9, © Shutterstock; 16–17 © Superstock; 19 © Ruby Tuesday Books; 29 © European Space Agency.

Library of Congress Cataloging-in-Publication Data

Owen, Ruth, 1967–
Venus / by Ruth Owen.
p. cm. — (Explore outer space)
Includes index.
ISBN 978-1-61533-723-1 (library binding) — ISBN 978-1-61533-763-7 (pbk.) —
ISBN 978-1-61533-764-4 (6-pack)
1. Venus (Planet)—Juvenile literature. 2. Venus (Planet)—Exploration—Juvenile literature. I. Title. II. Series: Owen, Ruth, 1967– Explore outer space.
QB621.O93 2014
523.42—dc23

2013004075

Manufactured in the United States of America

CPSIA Compliance Information: Batch #BS13WM: For Further Information contact Windmill Books, New York, New York at 1-866-478-0556

CONTENTS

THE BRIGHTEST PLANET

Look into the dark sky on a clear night and you will see a bright object that could be mistaken for a star. The shining, starlike object is actually a planet. It is Venus, our nearest planetary neighbor.

From Earth, Venus is the brightest planet in the **solar system**. It looks so bright to us because it is covered with yellowish-white clouds that reflect the Sun's light.

Venus formed at the same time and in the same way as Earth. It is nearly the same size as our planet and has a similar **mass**. Venus, however, is a very different world than our own.

If you could stand on Venus, the surface pressure would make it feel as if you were standing .5 mile (0.8 km) under the ocean. In fact, the pressure is so great that you would be crushed instantly. That would be, of course, if you hadn't already been burned to a crisp by temperatures that are hot enough to melt lead!

That's Out of This World!

The Romans named the five planets that could be seen in the night sky with the naked eye after their gods Mercury, Venus, Mars, Jupiter, and Saturn. The brightest planet was named for Venus, the goddess of love and beauty.

A Solar System Is Born

Venus, Earth, and the other planets in the solar system were created when our Sun formed about 4.5 billion years ago.

Before the solar system came into being, there was a huge cloud of gas and dust in space. Over time, the cloud collapsed on itself. Most of the gas and dust formed a massive spinning sphere, or ball. As the sphere spun in space, a disk formed around the sphere from the remaining gas and dust.

As all this matter rotated, the sphere pulled in more gas and dust, adding to its size, weight, and **gravity**. The pressure of all the material pressing onto the center of the sphere caused the center to get hotter and hotter. Finally, the temperature inside the sphere got so hot that the sphere ignited to become a new star. This new star was our Sun!

Inside the rotating disk, other masses formed. These became the solar system's planets, their **moons**, and smaller objects such as **asteroids**, **meteoroids**, and **comets**.

That's Out of This World!

Mercury, Venus, Earth, and Mars are the planets that formed closest to the Sun. All four planets have solid, rocky surfaces. They are known as the terrestrial planets. The word terrestrial comes from the Latin word terra, which means "earth" or "land."

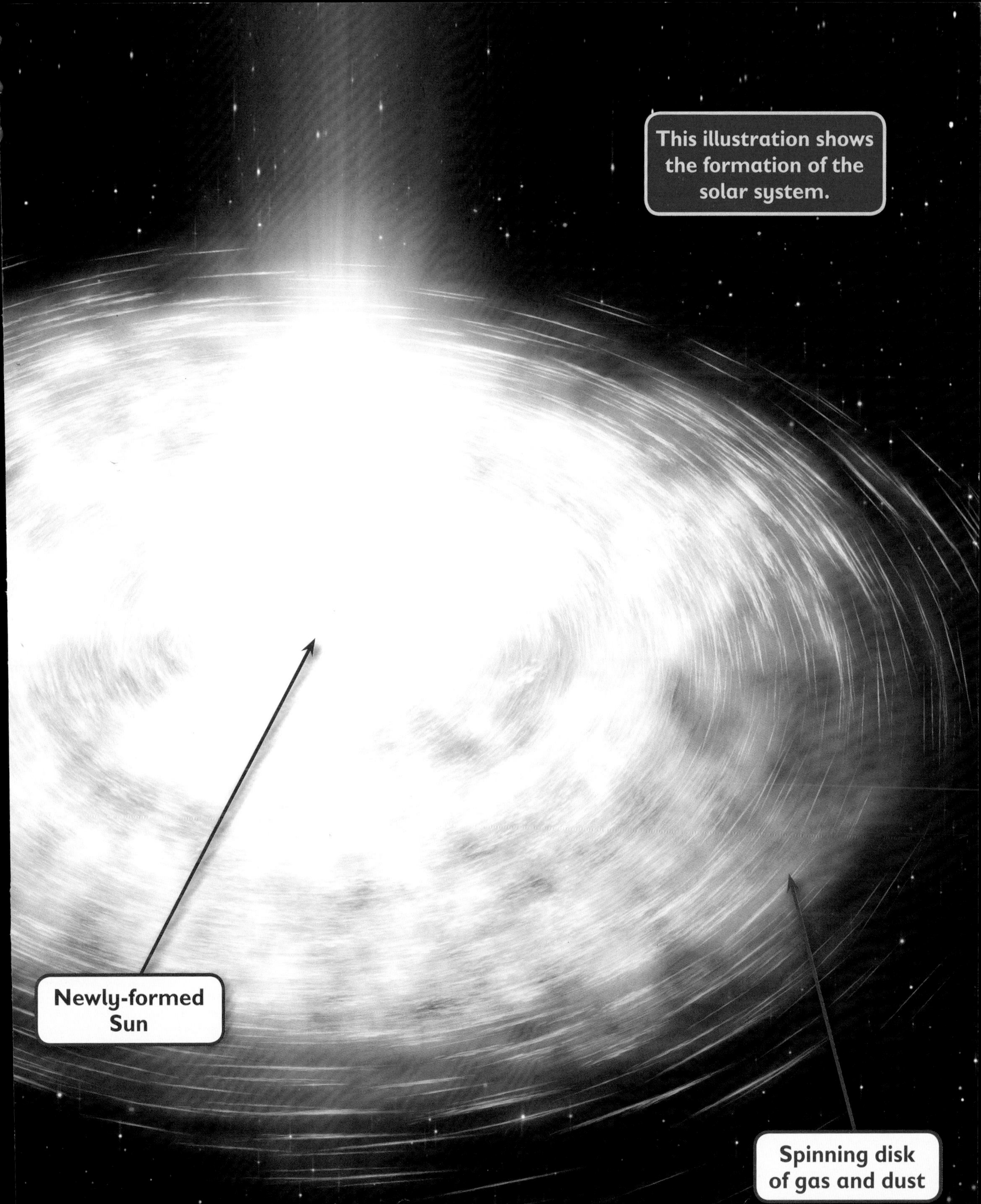
This illustration shows the formation of the solar system.
Newly-formed Sun
Spinning disk of gas and dust

OUR SOLAR SYSTEM

For around 4.5 billion years, the planets in our solar system have been orbiting the Sun, each taking its own path, or orbit, around our star.

Earth, the third planet from the Sun, takes 365 days to make one orbit. The more distant planets, however, take much longer. For example, Neptune makes one full orbit every 60,190 Earth days!

Five of the solar system's planets, Mercury, Venus, Mars, Jupiter, and Saturn, were known about from earliest times. Then, in March 1781, the British **astronomer** Sir William Herschel observed Uranus for the first time. At first, he thought he'd seen a comet. In September 1846, German astronomer Johann Gottfried Galle discovered Neptune, and in 1930, American astronomer Clyde Tombaugh discovered tiny, distant Pluto.

For decades our solar system was home to nine planets. Then, in 2006, The International Astronomical Union reclassified Pluto as a **dwarf planet** because of its small size. Also, it does not have the gravitational power to pull all the objects close to it into its orbit like the other "true" planets.

The Sun

This diagram shows our solar system. The planets' sizes in relation to each other and the distances between them are not to scale.

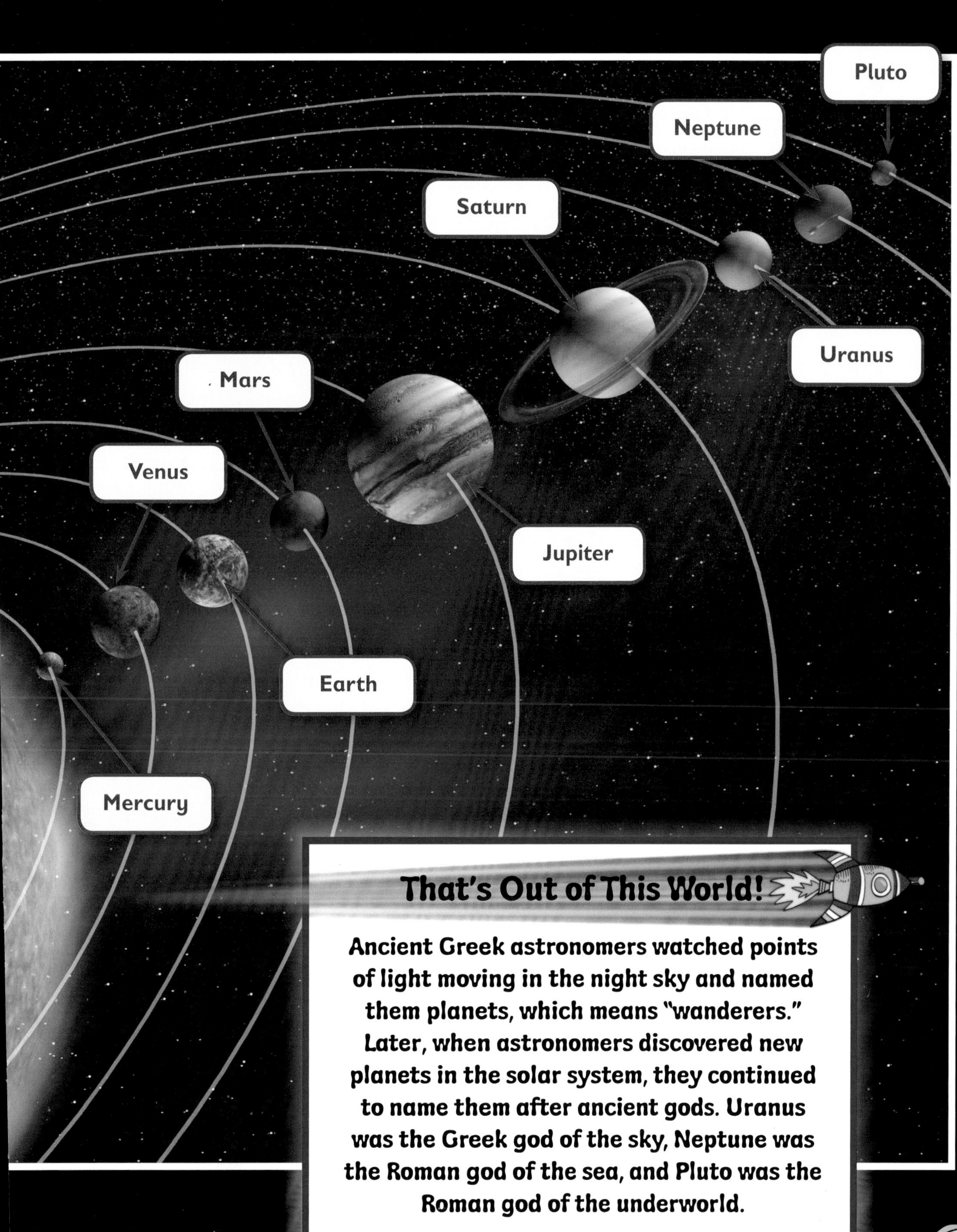

That's Out of This World!

Ancient Greek astronomers watched points of light moving in the night sky and named them planets, which means "wanderers." Later, when astronomers discovered new planets in the solar system, they continued to name them after ancient gods. Uranus was the Greek god of the sky, Neptune was the Roman god of the sea, and Pluto was the Roman god of the underworld.

Watching Venus

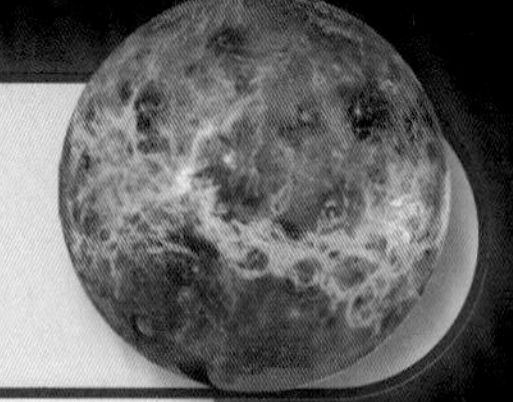

One of the ways that Venus can be seen from Earth is when it passes between Earth and the Sun. When this happens, Venus can be seen as a tiny black dot passing across the face of the Sun. This is called a transit.

Transits of Venus follow a predictable pattern. A transit will occur. Then, eight years later, it will happen again. Then, 121.5 years will pass by. Then two transits, separated by eight years, will again take place. Then, 105.5 years will pass before the next pair of transits, again separated by eight years. Then another 121.5 years must pass before the next transit, and so on and so on! The last transit of Venus happened in June 2012. Now, the world will not see this event again until the years 2117 and 2125.

In 1639, British astronomer Jeremiah Horrocks was the first person to view a transit of Venus. Horrocks directed an image of the Sun through his telescope onto a piece of paper so he could safely watch the transit without looking right at the Sun.

That's Out of This World!

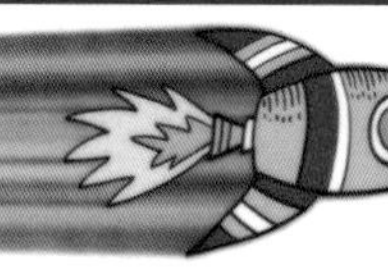

Jeremiah Horrocks used mathematical calculations and the 1639 transit of Venus to make an estimate of the distance from Earth to the Sun. He estimated the distance to be around 59 million miles (95 million km). Today, we know the Sun is 93 million miles (150 million km) away. However, Horrocks' original estimate was pretty good considering he wasn't using a computer or modern equipment!

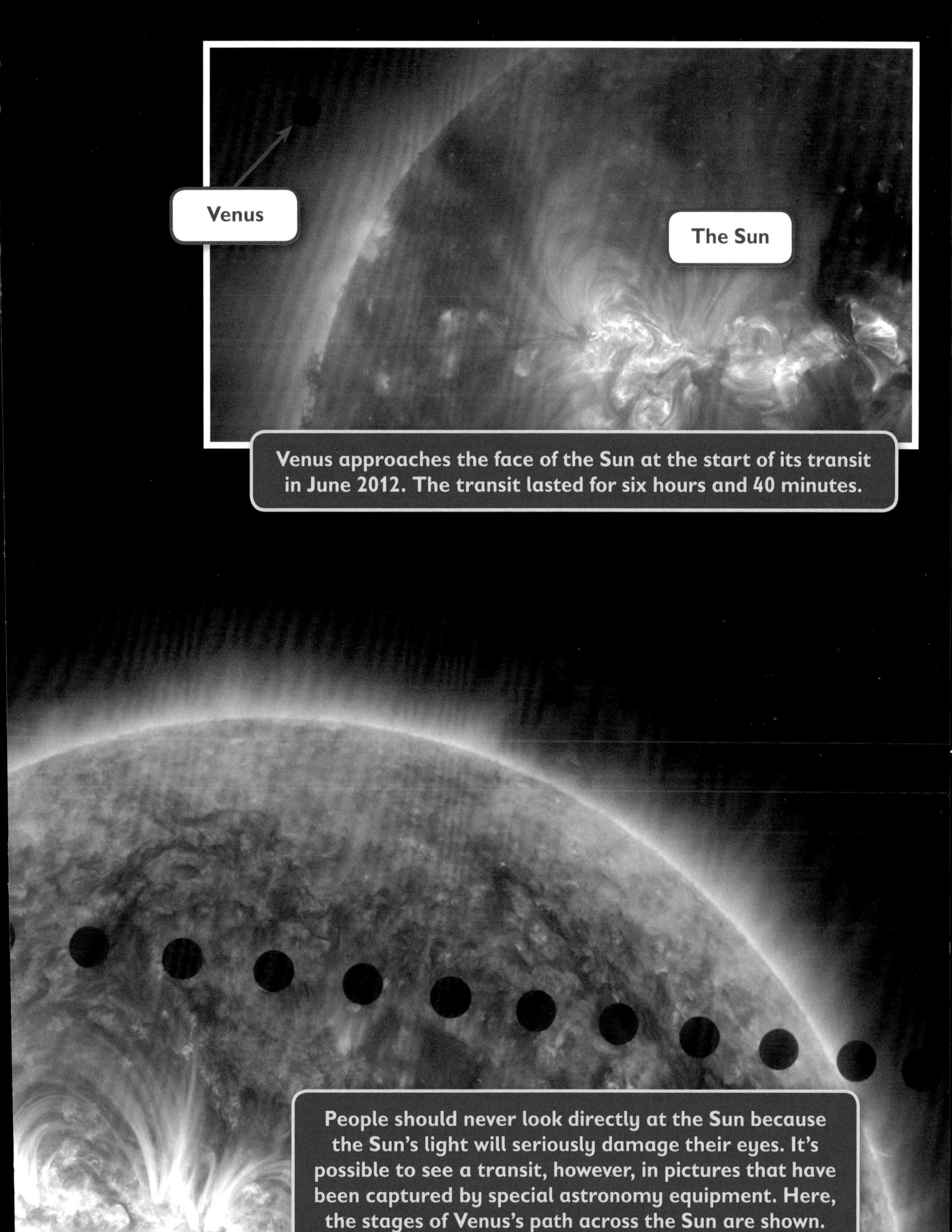

Venus approaches the face of the Sun at the start of its transit in June 2012. The transit lasted for six hours and 40 minutes.

People should never look directly at the Sun because the Sun's light will seriously damage their eyes. It's possible to see a transit, however, in pictures that have been captured by special astronomy equipment. Here, the stages of Venus's path across the Sun are shown.

VENUS'S DAYS AND YEARS

A year, or the time it takes Earth to make one full orbit of the Sun, lasts for 365 days. As Earth orbits, it also rotates, or turns, on its axis, making one full rotation every 24 hours. This is the time period that we call a day. Like Earth, Venus also has years and days.

To orbit the Sun, Earth makes a journey of nearly 560 million miles (900 million km). Venus is closer to the Sun, however, so its journey is shorter at just over 421 million miles (679 million km). This means that Venus can make one orbit of the Sun every 225 Earth days. So a year on Venus is 140 days shorter than on Earth.

Venus, however, rotates on its axis much slower than Earth. It takes 243 Earth days for Venus to make one full rotation.

That's Out of This World!

Venus not only rotates much slower than Earth, but it also rotates in the opposite direction. On Earth, we see the Sun rise in the east and set in the west. On Venus, it rises in the west and sets in the east.

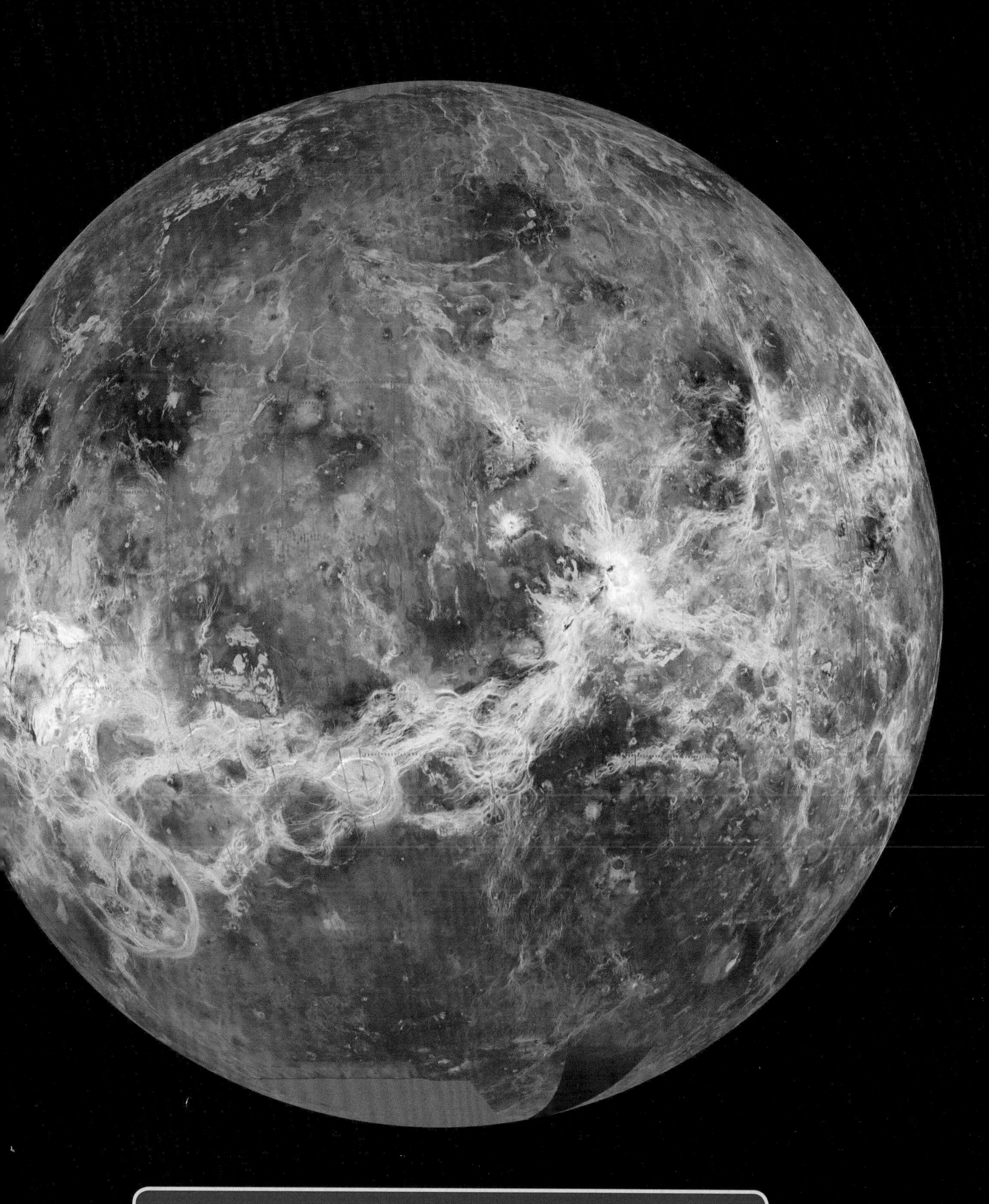

This beautiful image of Venus was created using computer-generated imagery and data and images captured by spacecraft that have visited the planet.

Venus, Inside and Out

The diameter of Venus is 7,520 miles (12,104 km) across. That's just 398 miles (641 km) smaller than the diameter of Earth.

Scientists think the interior of Venus is very similar to the layers of metal and rock that make up the inside of our planet. At the very center of Venus is a core of iron. Surrounding the core is a layer called the mantle, which is about 1,800 miles (2,900 km) thick. Like Earth's mantle, this layer of Venus is made up of rock and **molten** rock. The outer layer of the planet is a crust of rock that, in places, is 19 miles (30 km) deep.

Venus has slightly less mass than Earth, so the surface gravity on Venus is about 91 percent of the gravity on Earth. This means that if you weigh 100 pounds (45 kg) on Earth, you would weigh 91 pounds (41 kg) on Venus.

That's Out of This World!

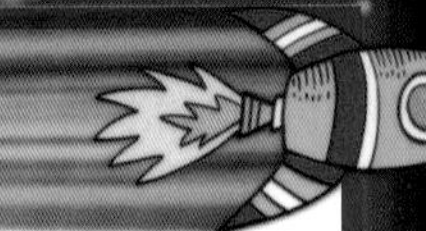

Venus's circumference at its equator is 23,627 miles (38,025 km) around. If you could drive a car at 60 miles per hour (97 km/h) without stopping, it would take just over 16 days to drive around Venus.

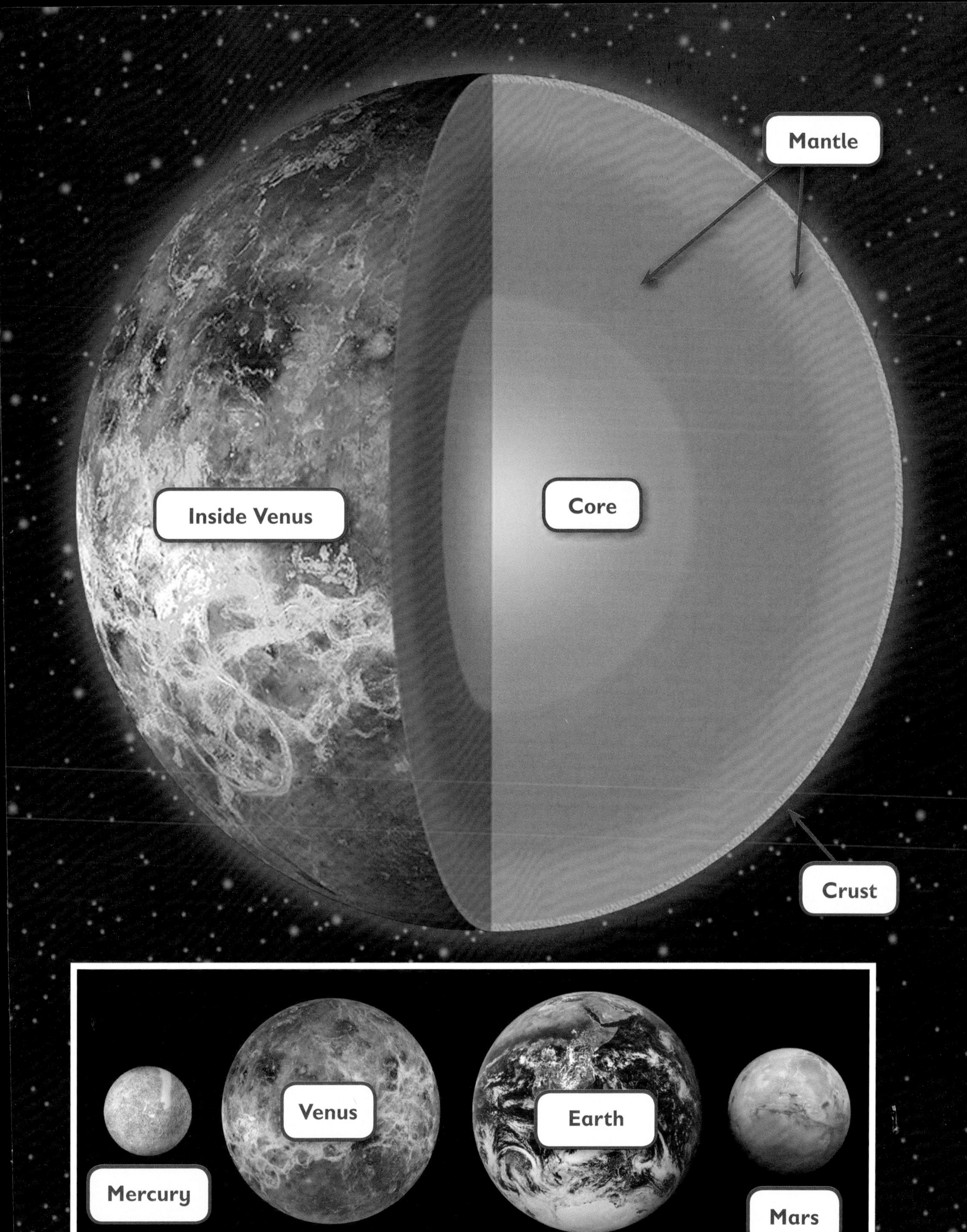

The relative sizes of the terrestrial planets

Venus's Atmosphere

Like its neighbor Earth, Venus is surrounded by a thick atmosphere made of gases.

Earth's atmosphere contains a mixture of gases, including oxygen, that make it possible for living things to breathe and survive on Earth. Venus's atmosphere is very different. It is made mostly of **carbon dioxide gas** with just a small quantity of nitrogen and traces of water vapor.

Above the dense layer of gases are thick clouds formed from **sulfur dioxide gas** and droplets of **sulfuric acid**. Venus's top layer of clouds hurtles around the planet driven by winds that travel at 220 miles per hour (350 km/h). These winds are far faster and stronger than most hurricane-force winds here on Earth! It is these clouds that give Venus a yellowish color. Bursts of lightning have also been detected coming from Venus's acid clouds. Closer to the planet's surface, the winds are far less fierce, traveling at just a few miles (km) per hour.

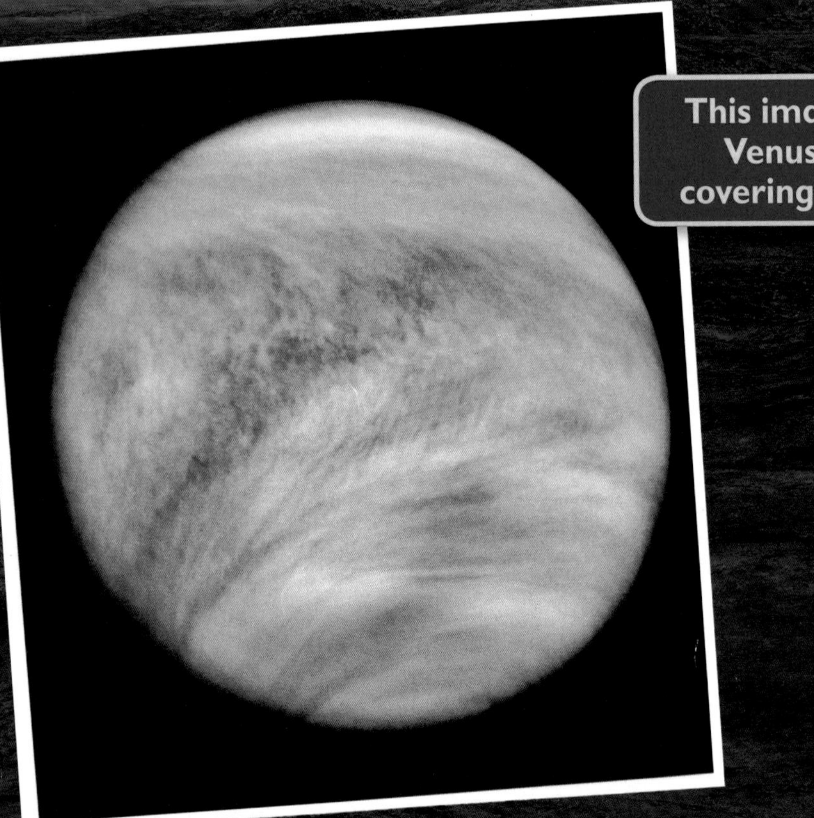

This image shows Venus's thick covering of clouds.

This illustration shows how the surface of Venus might look with the Sun's light blocked by the planet's dense atmosphere and blanket of poisonous clouds.

That's Out of This World!

Venus may be closer to the Sun than Earth, but its surface is not as well lit. The thick layer of gases and clouds surrounding the planet block out the Sun's light.

Scorching Venus

Venus is not the nearest planet to the Sun, but it is the hottest planet in the solar system. This is because of an effect that we also experience here on Earth called the greenhouse effect.

For decades, people on Earth have been burning fuels such as coal and oil. Burning these fuels releases gases such as carbon dioxide, methane, and nitrous oxide into Earth's atmosphere. These gases build up in the atmosphere and trap the Sun's heat on Earth, just as heat gets trapped in a greenhouse. This effect is known as the greenhouse effect, and on Earth it is causing temperatures to rise and **climate change** to happen. The greenhouse effect happens naturally on Earth, but human activities have added to it.

On Venus, the planet's naturally occurring carbon dioxide atmosphere also causes a greenhouse effect. Venus's atmosphere only allows about 10 percent of the Sun's heat through to the planet's surface. Once that heat is there, however, it is trapped by the thick blanket of carbon dioxide. This extreme greenhouse effect means that day or night, the temperature on the surface of Venus is a scorching 860 °F (460°C)!

That's Out of This World!

Venus's dense atmosphere reflects about 80 percent of the Sun's heat and light back into space. About 10 percent reaches the surface, and the other 10 percent is absorbed by the atmosphere.

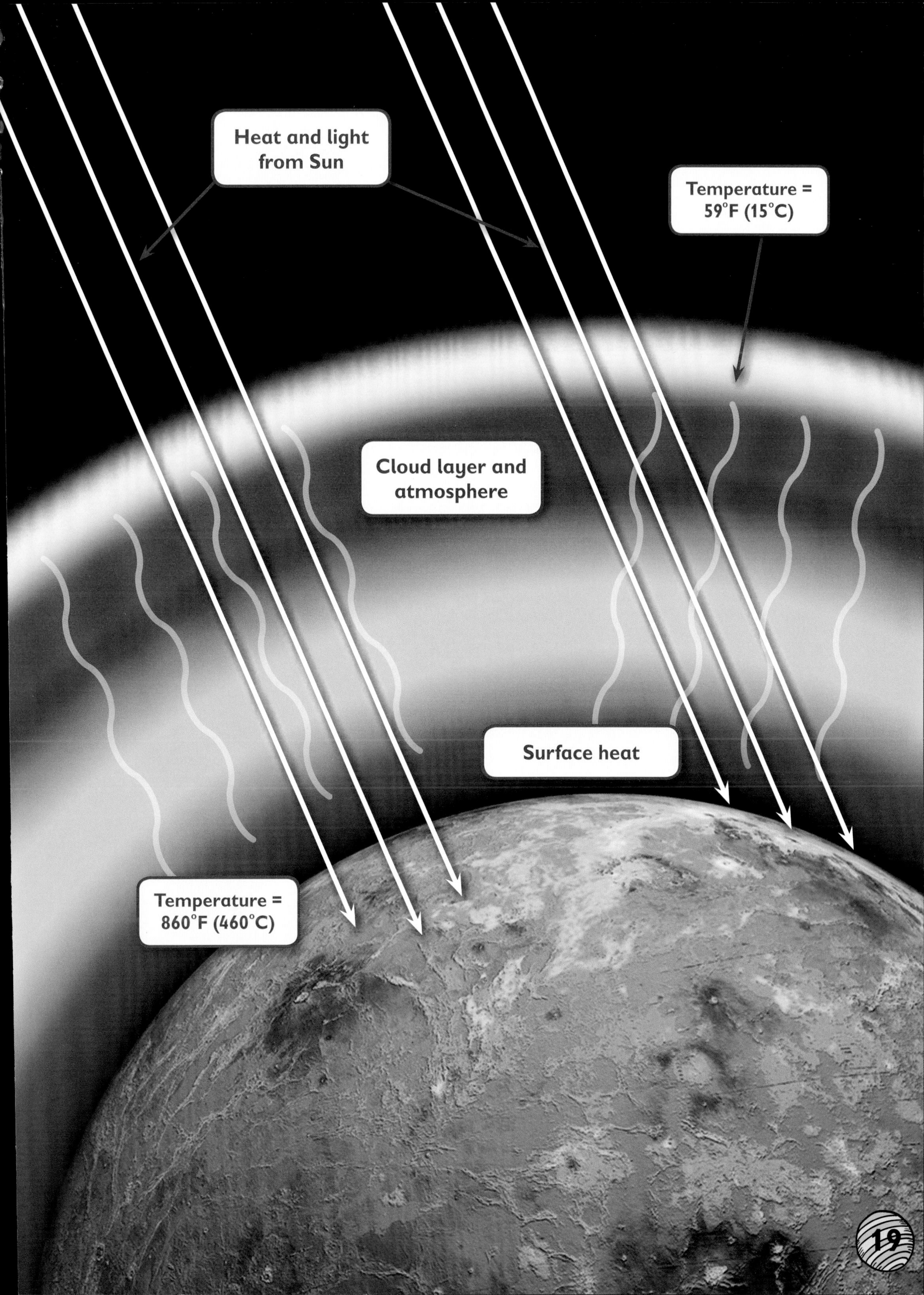
Heat and light
from Sun
Temperature =
59°F (15°C)
Cloud layer and
atmosphere
Surface heat
Temperature =
860°F (460°C)

SEEING THROUGH THE CLOUDS

Venus's thick covering of clouds makes it impossible to see the planet's surface with telescopes and equipment that use light waves. Radar, however, can penetrate the clouds and uses radio waves to "see" and create images.

Radar equipment sends out radio waves that bounce off an object, such as the surface of Venus. By analyzing the length of time it takes the wave to return and the length of the wave, radar equipment on Earth and aboard spacecraft that have visited the planet can create three-dimensional images. These images have been used to map Venus and reveal to us the planet's fascinating surface.

Images of Venus show a landscape of rolling plains, huge impact craters, mountains, and more than 1,000 volcanoes. Much of the planet's surface is covered with basalt rock. This rock forms when lava from inside a planet erupts onto the surface and then cools and hardens. Lava on Venus erupted from volcanoes and cracks in the planet's crust.

Crater

That's Out of This World!

Like all planets, Venus is sometimes on a collision course with space objects such as asteroids and meteoroids. Small meteoroids burn up as they enter the planet's thick atmosphere. Large objects may make it through, however, creating craters many miles (km) wide when they hit the planet's surface.

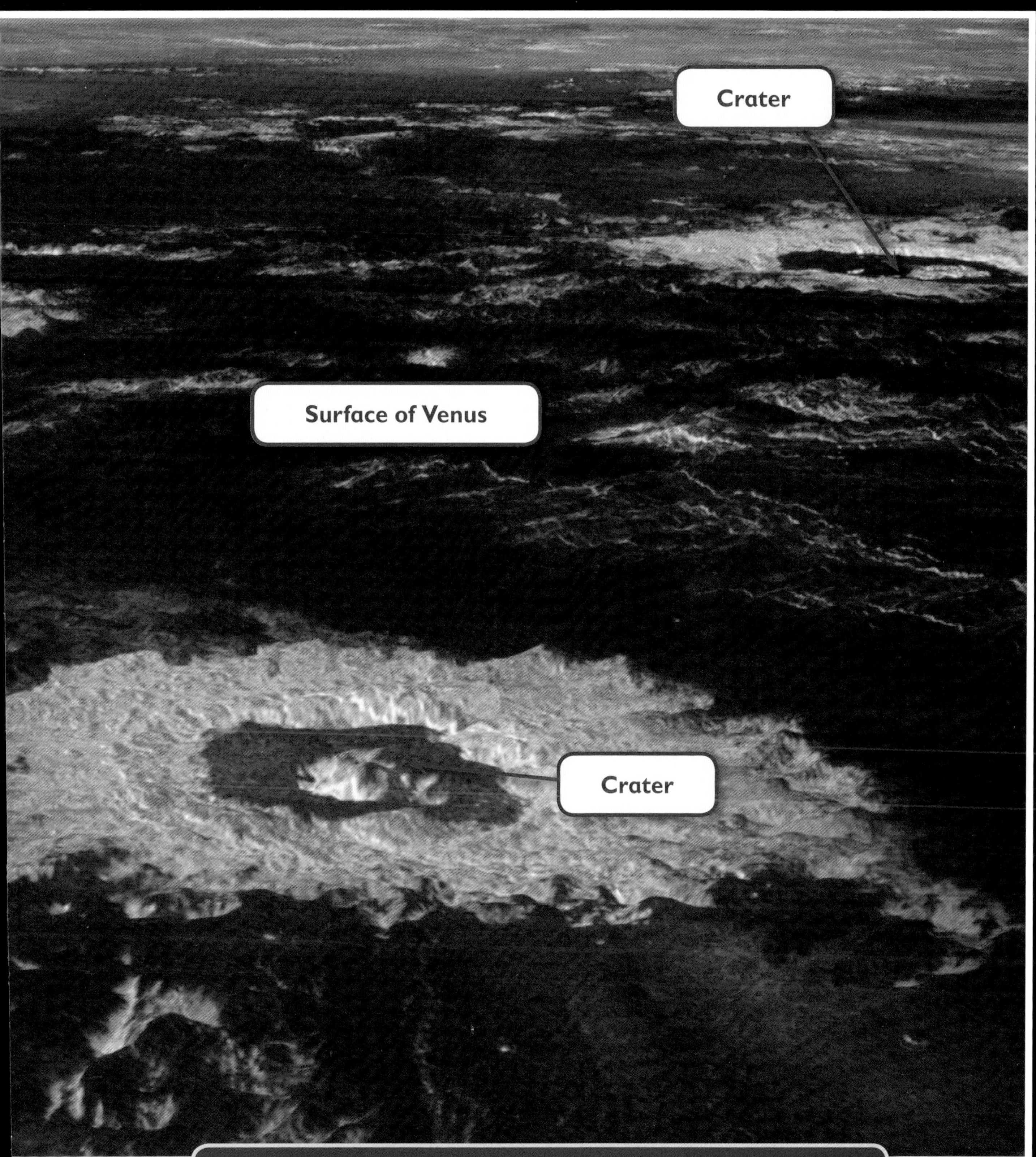

The craters in this image are part of an area of Venus's surface known as the crater farm. The crater in the foreground has a diameter of 23 miles (37 km).

MOUNTAINS AND VOLCANOES

Radar mapping of Venus has shown that the planet has two vast highland areas. One of these areas, named Ishtar Terra, is near the planet's north pole.

Ishtar Terra is an area larger than Australia. It is home to volcanoes and the planet's four main mountain ranges. Venus's tallest mountain, Maxwell Montes, is also in Ishtar Terra. Maxwell Montes is 7 miles (11 km) tall. That's about 1.5 miles (2.4 km) taller than Mount Everest, the tallest mountain on Earth.

Ishtar Terra is also home to many volcanoes. Some of the area's volcanoes are named for famous women from history, including Sacagawea and Cleopatra.

Venus has a history of volcanic eruptions, and it has been resurfaced many times by fresh lava flows over the billions of years of its lifetime.

This image shows Maxwell Montes from above. It is named for James Clerk Maxwell, a Scottish scientist whose work with radio waves made the invention of radar possible.

That's Out of This World!

Maat Mons is Venus's tallest volcano. At 5 miles (8 km) high, it stands nearly as tall as Mount Everest. The volcano was named for Maat, the ancient Egyptian goddess of truth and justice. Scientists do not believe that Maat Mons is active at the present time.

Radar imagery and computers were used to create this 3D image of the giant volcano Maat Mons. The lighter areas are lava flows that have cooled and solidified.

Exploring Venus

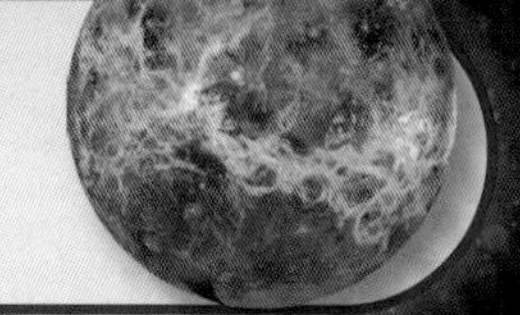

In 1962, NASA's *Mariner 2* became the first spacecraft to reach another planet and then send data back to Earth. Since *Mariner 2's* mission to Venus, many spacecraft have orbited and even landed on the planet.

From the early 1960s to early 1980s, the Soviet Union's Venera space program sent a series of spacecraft to Venus. The Venera program claimed many firsts for space exploration, and ten of the Venera spacecraft even landed on the planet's surface.

In 1967, *Venera 4* became the first spacecraft to enter the atmosphere of another planet. Then, in 1970, *Venera 7* was first to make a soft landing on another planet. In 1975, *Venera 9* was the first spacecraft to send pictures from another planet's surface back to Earth.

The spacecraft that landed on Venus did not survive for long before being destroyed by the heat and crushing surface pressure. *Venera 12*, which was sent to study Venus's atmosphere, survived the longest. It landed and then stayed in touch with Earth for 110 minutes.

This image of Venus's rocky surface was captured by *Venera 13*. This spacecraft was sent to Venus to study the planet's soil. The items at the bottom of the picture are parts of *Venera 13*.

This is the *Venera 13* landing craft. Venera is the Russian name for Venus.

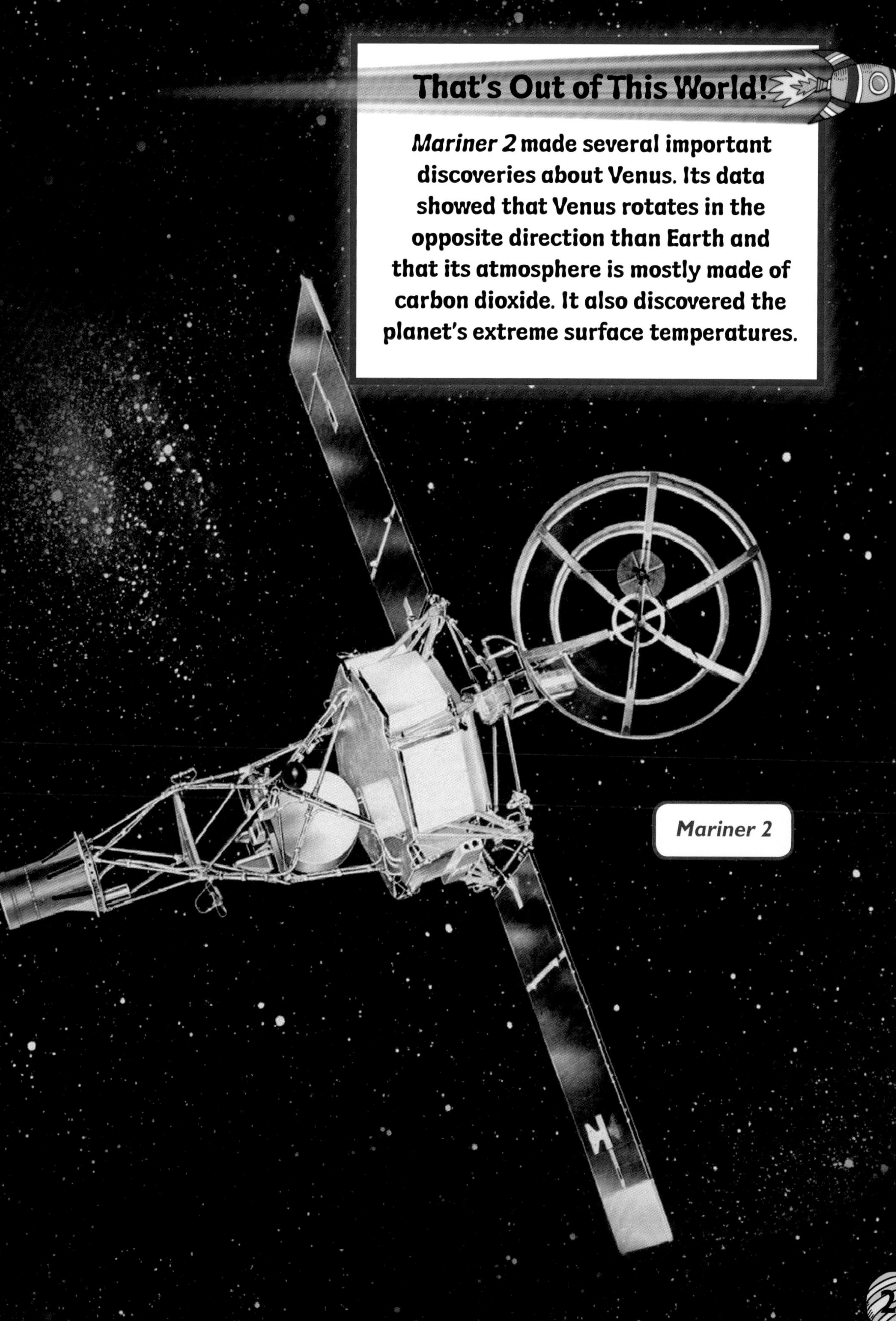

That's Out of This World!

Mariner 2 made several important discoveries about Venus. Its data showed that Venus rotates in the opposite direction than Earth and that its atmosphere is mostly made of carbon dioxide. It also discovered the planet's extreme surface temperatures.

Mariner 2

MAGELLAN

On May 4, 1989, the space shuttle *Atlantis* blasted off from Earth. Aboard was a robotic spacecraft named *Magellan.*

The following day, *Magellan* became the first spacecraft to be launched into space from a space shuttle. Fifteen months later, in August 1990, *Magellan* reached its destination and went into orbit around Venus.

Magellan's mission was to bounce radio waves off the planet's surface and transmit the results back to Earth. Images captured by *Magellan* showed surface winds, craters, and volcanoes. Its imagery showed that about 85 percent of Venus's surface is covered with ancient lava flows. Using radar, *Magellan* was able to create images of 98 percent of Venus's surface.

On October 12, 1994, the control crew on Earth gave *Magellan* its final command. It was to plunge into Venus's atmosphere. *Magellan* carried out its final task, transmitting data until it burned up. Its highly successful mission was over.

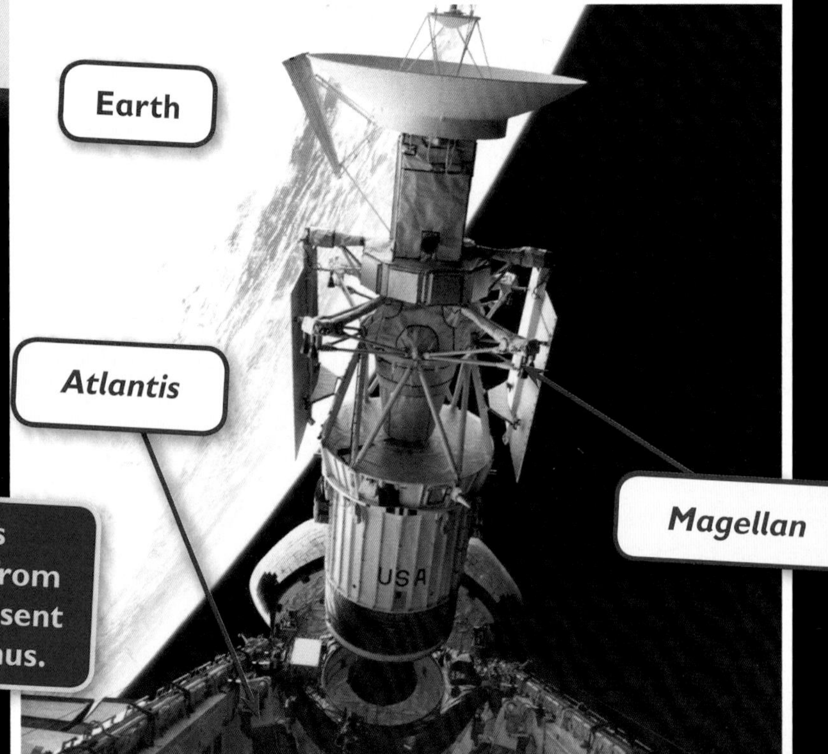

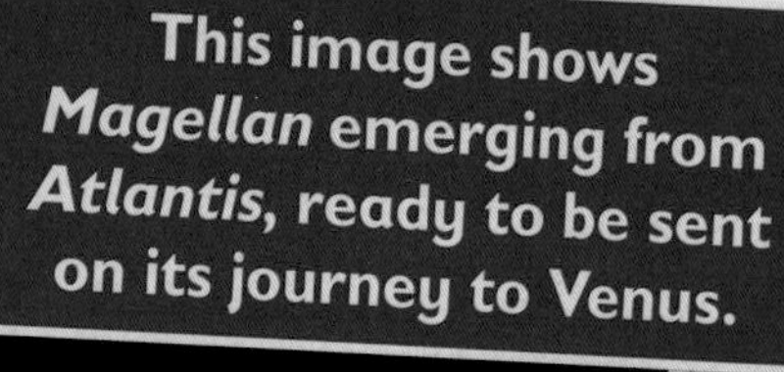
This image shows *Magellan* emerging from *Atlantis*, ready to be sent on its journey to Venus.

This image was created from a mosaic, or arrangement, of radar images captured by *Magellan* and radar equipment on Earth. The colors show the different heights of the surface features. Purples and blues represent low-lying ground. Pinkish-brown areas are high features such as mountains. Green areas are between the other two.

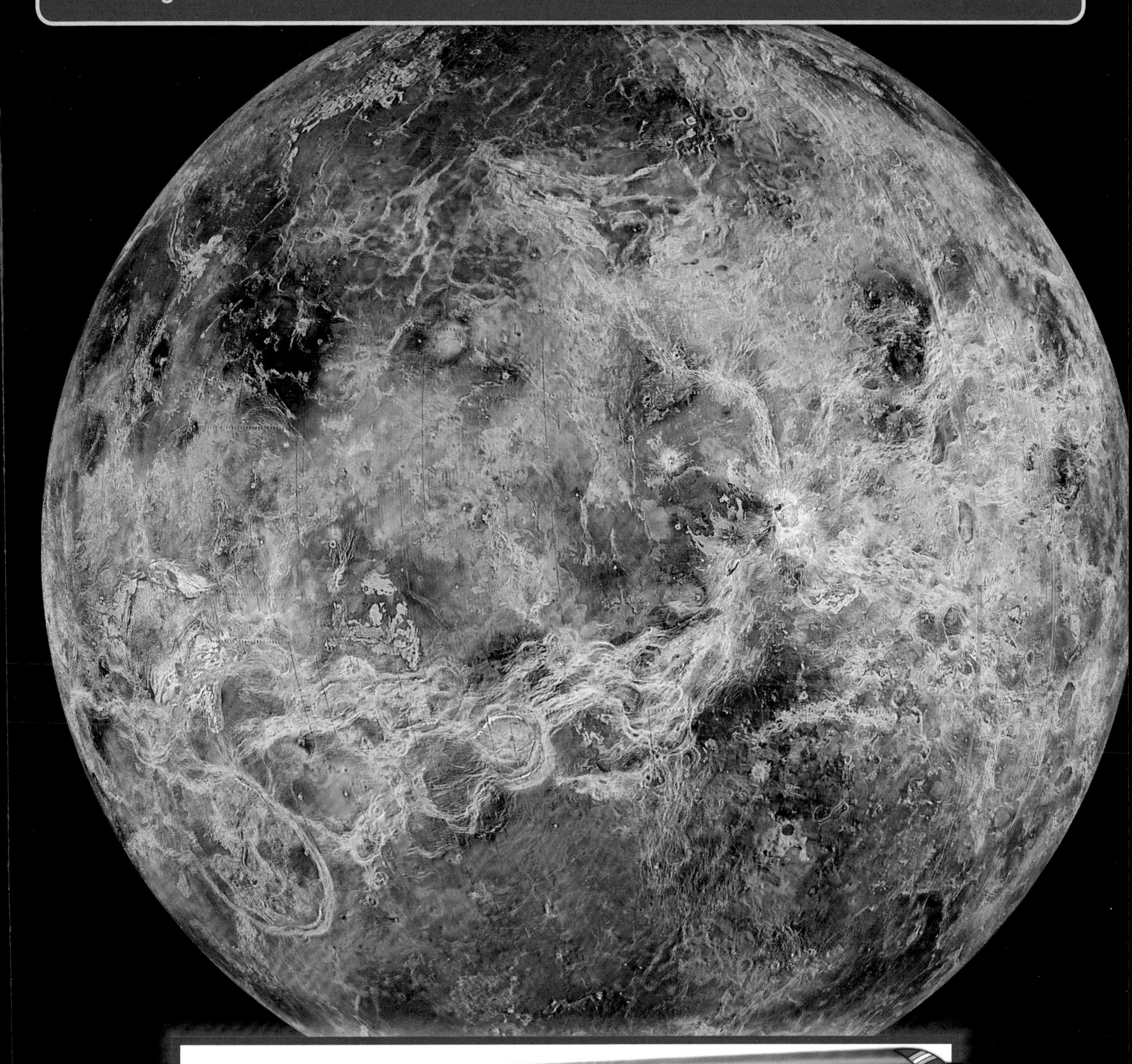

That's Out of This World!

The *Magellan* spacecraft was named after Ferdinand Magellan, a Portuguese explorer who was the first person to circumnavigate the world in the 1500s. The *Magellan* spacecraft is also known as the *Venus Radar Mapper*.

MYSTERIOUS VENUS

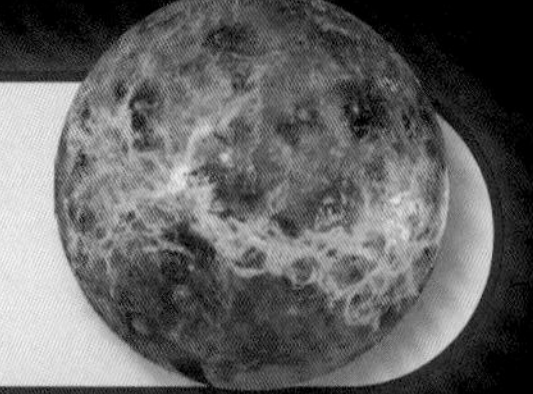

On November 9, 2005, the European Space Agency launched the *Venus Express* spacecraft. After a five-month-long journey through space, *Venus Express* went into orbit around Venus on April 11, 2006.

Venus Express was sent to study the planet's surface, volcanic activity, atmosphere, hurricane-force winds, and extreme greenhouse effect. It was also sent to examine the ways in which Venus and Earth are the same and different. One of its most exciting discoveries has been changes in the amount of sulfur dioxide in the upper atmosphere. Rising and then falling levels of this gas, which is produced by volcanoes, could mean that volcanic eruptions are still taking place on the planet's surface today.

Many spacecraft have visited Venus, but our superhot, mysterious neighbor still has lots of secrets to reveal. One of the biggest questions still to be answered is why a planet similar in size, and formed from the same materials as Earth, has developed into such a different world than our own over the past 4.5 billion years.

That's Out of This World!

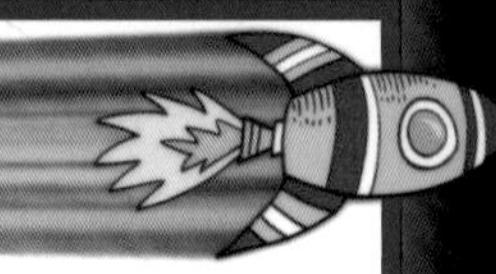

The body, or bus, of *Venus Express* is a box about 5 feet (1.5 m) wide. When its solar arrays are unfolded, the craft measures about 26 feet (8 m) wide. The solar arrays are winglike sections covered with solar cells, which absorb the Sun's energy and use it to power the spacecraft.

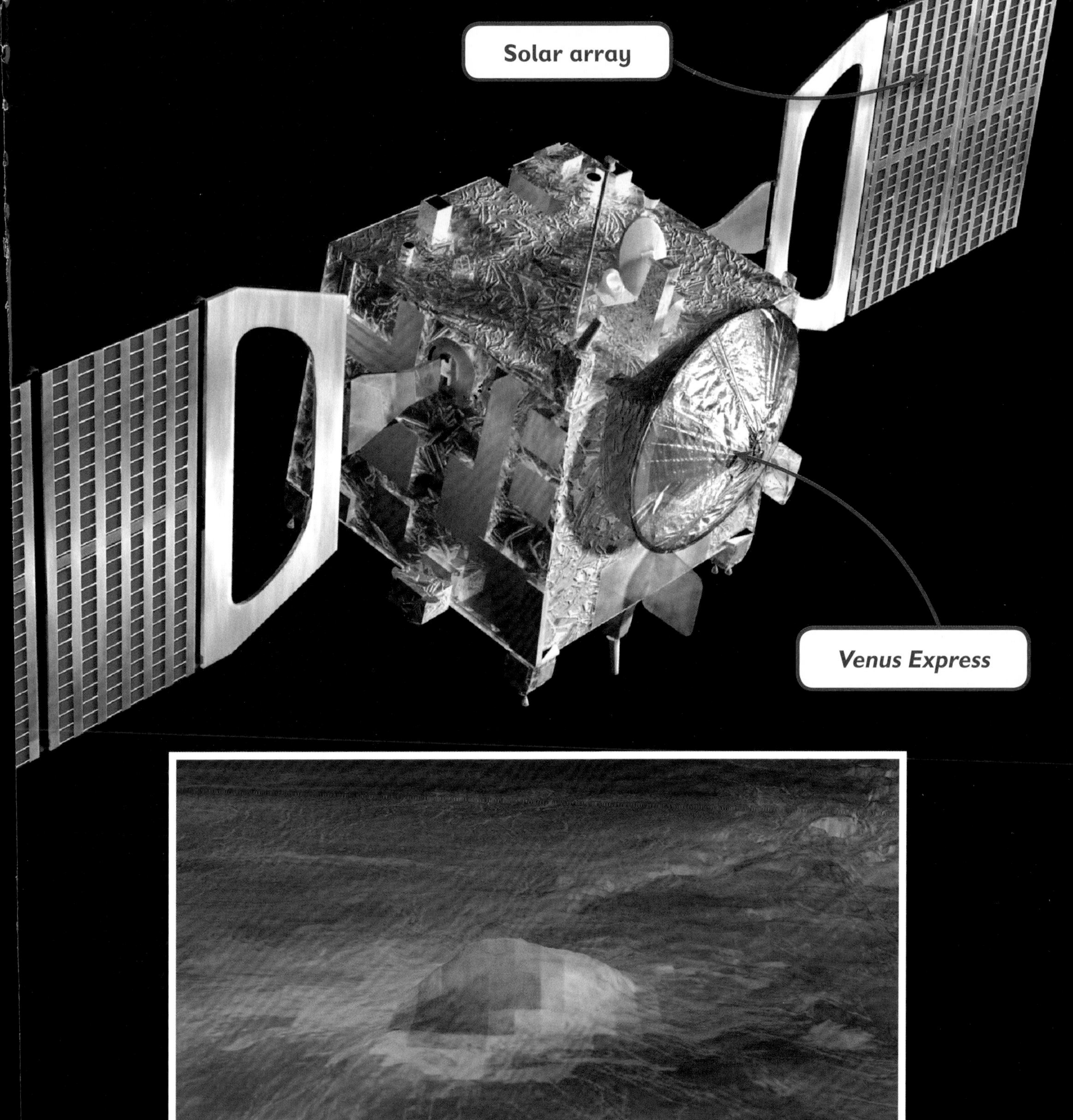

This image shows Idunn Mons, a volcano on Venus. The colors in the image show the age of the surface features. The orange is the youngest material. It is possibly that lava has recently flowed from the volcano.

GLOSSARY

asteroid (AS-teh-royd) Rocky objects orbiting the Sun and ranging in size from a few feet (m) to hundreds of miles (km) in diameter.

astronomer (uh-STRAH-nuh-mer) A scientist who specializes in the study of outer space.

atmosphere (AT-muh-sfeer) The layer of gases surrounding a planet, moon, or star.

axis (AK-sus) An imaginary line about which a body, such as a planet, rotates.

carbon dioxide gas (KAHR-bun dy-OK-syd GAS) A naturally occurring gas found in the atmosphere of several planets. On Earth, humans and other animals release carbon dioxide when they breathe out. It also comes from volcanoes and the burning of fuels that contain carbon, such as coal and oil.

circumnavigate (SER-kem-NA-vuh-gayt) To travel all the way around something, such as an island, a continent, or the entire Earth.

climate change (KLY-mut CHAYNJ) The gradual change in temperatures on Earth. For example, the current warming of temperatures caused by a buildup of greenhouse gases in the atmosphere.

comets (KAH-mits) Objects orbiting the Sun consisting primarily of a nucleus, or center, of ice and dust and, when near the Sun, tails of gas and dust particles pointing away from the Sun.

dwarf planet (DWAHRF PLA-net) An object in space that looks and acts like a planet but is much smaller.

equator (ih-KWAY-tur) An imaginary line drawn around a planet that is an equal distance from the north and south poles.

gravity (GRA-vuh-tee) The force that causes objects to be attracted toward Earth's center or toward other physical bodies in space, such as stars, planets, and moons.

greenhouse effect (GREEN-hows eh-FEKT) The warming of a planet's surface and atmosphere due to heat from the Sun trapped in the planet's atmosphere by a layer of gases called greenhouse gases.

mass (MAS) The quantity of matter in a physical body that causes it to have weight when acted upon by gravity.

meteoroids (MEE-tee-uh-roydz) Small particles or fragments that has broken free from an asteroid.

molten (MOHL-ten) Melted, or liquefied, by heat.

moons (MOONZ) Natural objects that orbit a planet.

orbiting (OR-bih-ting) Circling in a curved path around another object.

planet (PLA-net) An object in space that is of a certain size and that orbits, or circles, a star.

radar (RAY-dahr) An electronic system that can detect the shape, size, and distance of objects by bouncing radio waves off them and analyzing the waves when they are reflected back.

solar system (SOH-ler SIS-tem) The Sun and everything that orbits around it, including planets and their moons, asteroids, meteors, and comets.

space shuttle (SPAYS SHUH-tul) A winged spacecraft that can be launched into Earth orbit with its crew and equipment to perform missions in space, return to Earth in a runway landing, and be reused for other missions. NASA, the US space agency, operated the space shuttle program between 1982 and 2011.

star (STAR) A body in space that produces its own heat and light through the release of nuclear energy created within its core.

sulfur dioxide gas (SUL-fur dy-OK-syd GAS) A naturally occurring poisonous gas that is released by volcanoes and can also be released by burning coal and petroleum.

sulfuric acid (sul-FYUR-ik A-sid) A colorless, oily liquid that can seriously damage many materials, including flesh.

WEBSITES

For web resources related to the subject of this book, go to: www.windmillbooks.com/weblinks and select this book's title.

Read More

Hughes, Catherine D. *National Geographic Little Kids First Big Book of Space.* Des Moines, IA: National Geographic Children's Books, 2013.

Landau, Elaine. *Venus.* A True Book. Danbury, CT: Children's Press, 2008.

Stott, Carole. *Space Exploration.* New York: DK Children, 2010.

Index